BRAID

THE NEVER AFTERS

BRAID

A NEVER AFTERS TALE

KIRSTYN MCDERMOTT

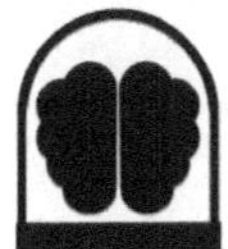

Brain Jar Press
PO Box 6687
Upper Mt Gravatt, QLD, 4122
Australia
www.BrainJarPress.com

Cover design by Peter Ball
Cover Image: *Woman's Braid,* GrigoryL/Shutterstock

ISBN: 978-1-922479-99-0 (Ebook) | 978-1-922479-98-3 (Chapbook)

BRAID

Winter makes me think of the tower. Even now, after all this time. Trapped here in the valley for these months of snow and ice. Unable to pack up and leave at will, no matter how much my spirit chafes at being made still. There's a world waiting past those spiny mountain ridges and I ache to move within it.

Gryff likes the winter. His restless years are winding down, he says, and he looks forward to laying his bones in the same place each night. For many nights. He looks forward to evenings in the village mead hall. To the drinking and telling of tales, tall and not so tall. We're safe here, he tells me, we've always been safe here. Would it be so dull to settle for a time, to spend a year or three watching the seasons change in this little valley?

Watching our great-grandson grow?

He still wishes for it to be a boy, Willa's baby. I'm certain it's a girl; she's carrying so high. Willa thinks so too. She wants to call her Chance. I've said nothing, though it weighs badly on me. Willa's headstrong, like her mother was — is, like her mother is. If I take against it, the name will stick faster than flyrot. The child, she thinks, was seeded by the spice trader from the south; the timing lends itself to him at least. She always speaks of the man fondly. His thighs, long and taut. His kind eyes. But theirs was no more than a summer cleaving, as bright and as brief as the courtship of fireflies.

I hope she has his sweet brown eyes, Willa has said more than once. I hope her heart is kind.

The dark bay mare whickers as I near the stables, water bucket in hand. She'll drop her own baby come spring, a foal we've promised to Boorma. We've camped in the yard beside her home for several winters and she's always vouchsafed us to the village circle. I want to do this for her. I want the dark bay mare to stay fat and happy. I want the foal to be born healthy. Strong. Steady on its hooves.

The bucket barely fills the water trough a quarter way. The mare has been thirsty overnight; I'll need to bring more from the well, or else send Boorma's son. He's young and strong and can carry a full bucket in each hand. I fork fresh hay into her feed bin. She pushes at me to get past, her big head knocking me off kilter. My feet slip in the semi-frozen mud and I snatch a handful of mane to keep from falling. The mare pays me no mind. If I break my leg, I tell her, you will starve to death. It's not true. No one in the village would allow a good broodmare to starve, especially not one with a belly full of legs.

A flash of unseasonal colour catches my eye and I turn, almost falling again when I spot the bird perched on the railing outside. It's about the size of a hill pigeon but with plumage the colour of precious jewels. Sapphires, emeralds and rubies, all a-gleam in the weak morning sun. I haven't seen its like since I was a girl.

Silvery stitches run the length of its breast. Not ordinary twine or thread, I see as I move closer, but a thin strand of hair. Deep in my bones, I know that hair was once a bright, burnished auburn and that it curled in waves down to wide and comfortable hips. I can hear laughter, throaty and warm. I can see narrowed eyes, wet with anger and hurt.

The bird allows me to pick it up and turn it over onto its back. Its stitches pull loose with a tug, and that beautiful blue breast opens.

Inside, the creature is hollow and black. But not empty.

The ring is just as I remember it. That thick silver band. That huge, smooth-polished moonstone. Deceptively plain, unlike the woman who used to wear it. My stomach tightens; the cup of warmed goat's milk I had for breakfast curdles within me. She always wore this ring. Always. She wouldn't have taken it off while there was still breath in her body. Or only when there was breath just enough.

The bird now hangs limp in my hand. The silver hair has turned dull and brittle, its magic spent.

Picking up the bucket, I drop the feathered corpse into it then run a slow, shaky hand over the mare's belly. Good girl, I tell her, good little mother. The steps I take back to camp are equally slow, equally shaky. Beneath the cap Willa knitted for me, my scalp crawls. Wisps of greying hair escape and catch in my mouth. I've kept my hair cropped short for more than three decades, much to Gryff's sorrow. I see the disappointment in his eyes each time I take up the shears. Long hair is trouble, I tell him. You of all men should appreciate that.

At the door to our yurt, I pause, heart racing despite my steady pace. As long as I don't see, as long as I don't *know*, the world can remain unchanged. But what kind of fool would I be to make such a wish? I spit onto the ground. Rub it into the muddy snow, the toe of my boot moving widdershins, and mutter a blessing.

Inside, Willa is still sitting by the stove, still at her knitting. She looks up as I come in, a smile faltering on her lips. Mother Zel? she asks. What's wrong? At the sound of my name, the thick golden braid coiled in her lap stirs and slides noiselessly to the floor. It covers the distance between us in less time than it takes for me to draw a single deep breath and curls itself about my ankles. I drop the bucket and gather it into my arms, pressing my face into that warm, silken hair. The braid smells as it always has: of springtime and sunshine and safety. A half-strangled sob escapes my tightening throat.

Mother Zel? Willa asks again. Her voice trembles.

Gothel is dead, I tell her. Dead or so near it makes no matter.

I hug the braid close. Coiled about my waist and shoulders, it squeezes gently in return. My knees weaken and I sink to a crouch. How I feared to find it changed, reduced to something as lifeless and spent as those stitches I pulled from the bird. It came from Gothel's magic, after all. How long can it survive her death? In my worry, I've forgotten to close the door and now a chill wind sneaks across the threshold. My granddaughter heaves herself from her chair. I'll fetch Boorma, she tells me.

I nod. Tell her to find Gryff. Please.

She sidles past, her rounded belly brushing my shoulder. She pauses for a moment, her breath catching as she stares no doubt at the contents of the bucket, before pushing the door shut behind her. It's quiet in the yurt, and still. The braid nudges the hollow of my throat, presses against my cheek. I know, I whisper, I know.

People know the tales about Mother Gothel, or think they do. Some grew from my own words, my own past relayed to the wise woman who first took pity on me, windblown and pregnant, soon after my exile all those years ago. Her joints beginning to creak with age, she allowed me a straw-filled mattress and what food she could spare in return for feeding her goats and collecting the eggs from her motley flock of chickens each morning. It made for a rude change from the tower, but the smell of feathers and warm shell comforts me to this day. In the evenings, I told her about Gothel, about her wild, wondrous garden and the tower in which my most recent years were spent, about my impossibly long hair and the iron shears that had cropped it from my skull.

Gothel is a witch, the wise woman told me. And I should know.

She calls herself an enchantress, I said.

The wise woman shrugged. Witch, enchantress, healer, crone. Names only matter to those what wield them as weapons, girlie. Rest of us prefer plain-speaking to fancy talk.

I told her about my prince as well. At the time, I had no idea what had happened to him but feared the worst. If Gothel could turn on me so savagely, shear the hair in which she had taken such pride, send me with a blink to this strange and desolate land, what would she have done to him next he came calling? Worrying kept me awake most nights, at least until the twins were born and my days became filled to exhaustion. Chance, I named the girl, and the boy was Will. Both had dark brown hair and big green eyes so like their father's it made me weep.

Don't fret on him, the wise woman told me. He'll have found some other lass to woo by now. A princess, most like, or some fine lady, if he's what you say he is.

But he hadn't, and he wasn't.

The twins were only a moon off their second birthday, the day Gryff dragged his blinded self to our door. It was your singing, he told me. Your sweet voice drew me here sure as the north star.

Which might have been part of the truth, but wasn't the whole. It was the braid, my braid, that led him to me. He told me about climbing the tower that final time and how his eagerness for our time together was dashed by Gothel's triumphant sneer. He told me about the rose bushes below and how they took his eyes as greedily as a child plucks fruit from a pudding. I remembered the rose bushes and their perfume that drifted to my window on warm, windswept afternoons. I remembered their sharp and wicked thorns.

Mother Gothel pushed you? I asked.

Gryff hesitated. I fell, he said. I was shocked to see her and I slipped. She didn't touch me.

I loved him for that small honesty, when so easily he could have lied. I love him for it still.

He had wandered for less than a week, or so he figured, before the braid found him. He knew it was mine. It smelled like me and, besides, who else in the world had ever hair long enough to cover the whole of his body on those frostbitten nights when temperatures plummeted to freezing? The braid nudged him and nuzzled him and kept him moving when he felt like crawling into a hole, covering himself with dirt, and coughing his last. It nosed out fresh water in unexpected crevices and found wild berries and mushrooms which he ate in greedy handfuls. Day after footsore day, he followed the braid until they came at last upon the wise woman's cottage. When he heard me singing a song he remembered from the tower, he could barely breathe for joy.

I know the tales they tell about my tears. How they spilled with love and wonder onto my prince's face and made whole his poor, damaged eyes. I did weep over him, that's true enough. We wept together, the two of us, but it was my braid that worked the magic. It curled itself around us, brushing against our cheeks and mingling our tears. Then it flicked itself across Gryff's eyes, once and once again, and his lids fluttered open and his brilliant green irises stared, astonished, into my own.

I thought I would never see you again, he croaked. I thought I would never see.

My dear prince, I said, come meet your children.

Gryff wasn't a prince, of course, mine or anyone else's. On the night of our reunion, as our fingers explored bodies grown unfamiliar and strange, he told me the truth. Not a prince but the third son of a bankrupt lord. There was no throne awaiting him, no inheritance and certainly no line of fine ladies jostling for a ring.

You asked if I were a prince, sweet Zel, that first day I came to the tower.

And you said that you were.

It felt like a game, or a dream. The tower felt like a place for dreams.

Not for me, Gryff.

Then we fell in love, he said, and it was too late. I didn't know how to tell you. He rested his head on my shoulder. His hair was damp and smelled of lavender from the bath I'd given him earlier. Do you still love me, he asked, even if I have no kingdom to offer?

I kissed his brow. I kissed each of his eyes in turn. It was never a kingdom I wanted, I said. And then I kissed his mouth, deeply, hungrily, as a princess never would.

It might have been the wise woman who planted the seeds, spreading stories of my healing powers to further her own standing, but I have cultivated them mercilessly. Though I've only one tenth of Gothel's power, I'm a quick learner and reputation makes up for a lot. No one knows about my braid, and the magic contained within its strands, save a handful of trusted souls. In all my life, I've only used it twice. Once, when Will burned for three nights straight with marsh fever and the second, years later, to save my daughter's life. She's never thanked me for that, nor forgiven me.

Boorma believes that our lives are fated to unfurl as they will. Just because we can't see the path ahead of us, she says, doesn't mean there isn't a path. Take your steps and trust where your feet lead you. I don't agree, a stand which has given rise to many a gentle argument over the years. I think that we make our path as we go, and that each and every footfall could have so easily landed at a different angle, skewed our direction, turned us completely about. Sometimes, I look back at all the steps I've taken and a deep longing churns my stomach. In my head a voice whispers, if only. If only. The voice sounds like Gothel's. Or it sounds like my daughter's. If only.

If only I had turned away from the pearl house that awful summer when the world tilted slantwise. If only I had galloped back to the hillside where my family was making camp. If only we had all packed up and left. That step. That moment. That choice. But what would be lost to make it anew? Willa, most certainly, and the baby with her — and there it begins and ends. I will not play this game. If only. If only. It doesn't matter, none of it. Our paths may not be fixed but, once forged, they're irrevocable.

Mind your steps instead, I tell Boorma, and know when to stop walking in the first place.

Our own advice, of course, is always the hardest to follow.

Not a month passes that I don't think of that summer, the last that Boorma travelled with us, the last my family would spend unbroken. I'd been so eager to see Heggu before dusk I left Gryff and the twins to unload the wagon and set up our shelters. Boorma was already nursing her new baby and she raised one arm as I trotted away, calling out for me to pass on her good wishes to Heggu. The chestnut gelding was sulky, resenting the extra length to his day while our other two horses were happily grazing in their hobbles, and I dug my heels hard into his sides. By the time we reached Heggu's little cottage by the lake, the beastly nag was tossing his head so violently that my hands were chafed from reining him in.

It was the first sign, but I failed to heed it.

Cursing, I slid from his back and yanked him over to the tether-line. It looked ill-maintained, the overhead rope mossy and close to fraying. I tied the chestnut gelding to an end-post instead. I should have thought more about the state of the line, and how odd it was that no horse seemed to have been tied to it for months, but I was tired and cranky and looking forward to Heggu's lavender tea. It was the sight of her door that first gave me pause. This early in summer, it should have been decorated by a garland of wildflowers, strung on horsehair with a pearl or two hidden among the petals. Or, at the very least, a bushel of dried lakeweed offered in expectation of the oyster harvest. The bare wood troubled me, as did the rusty, unadorned nail. I pushed open the door.

The cottage was empty, and had been for some time. Instead of the aroma of woodsmoke and cooking grease, the place smelled musty and close. The round glass window — a particular point of pride for Heggu — was half-obscured by cobwebs. It hadn't been cleaned in months. But there was no sign of abandonment, nor ransacking. Whatever had happened, Heggu had found time to pack up her most personal belongings before she left. Most of the drawers in her wooden cabinet were barren, but the secret compartment at the back held a small cotton bag. Pearl dust, by the weight and chalky smell of it, the very thing I came to trade with her each summer.

Blessed by three, I muttered, dropping the bag into my pocket. Thank you, Heggu.

It was only when I turned to go did I notice what else she'd left for me. On the back of the door hung an ornate sigil, woven from dried plains-grass and the weed that grew near her oyster beds. She'd woven it herself over many months and had taken the time one summer to tell me the meaning of it. Not the whole meaning — some knowledge was meant for only Heggu herself

— but enough. It was the story of her life, and the places she had lived over the years, and the lessons she had learnt. Except now it was the wrong way around, the hook stuck rudely through a piece of weave on its lowest arc rather than the loop she had fashioned to hang it from.

The world, Heggu's world, had been turned upside down.

I couldn't leave it like that. But as soon as my fingers touched the sigil there was a spark, like the small shocks that come from brushing long hair on a dry summer day, and a whisper that I heard more in my head than my ears.

run

Clutching Heggu's sigil to my chest — silent now and still, no more than dead grass — I fled the cottage. But it was too late to run any farther.

Waiting outside were four men on horses, one of them holding my chestnut gelding by its rope. I recognised three of them from the nearby village. The fourth man was thin and tall, even for sitting on his mount, with a narrow face and eyes that seemed like they could be kind when they wanted to be. One of the others, a man I knew as Jacoby, shifted in his saddle. His wife had been pregnant last summer and sick more mornings than not. I'd given her a tincture, told her to roll a pearl under her tongue when she needed to be on her feet. She would've had the baby by now. A son, or so I'd reckoned at the time.

That's her, Jacoby said, lifting his chin. That's the witch.

By the time the door to the yurt opens again, I've gathered myself together. There's a pot of water coming to boil on the stove and I'm sitting in my chair, cutting up root vegetables on a board in my lap. The braid is curled around my feet and ankles. It stirs as Willa comes in then settles itself again. Willa asks how I am. I tell her that I'm almost done with the turnips but that we need more sweet potato for the soup. Her smile is weak and worried. She glances into the bucket left by the door.

In here, I say, kicking a heel against the basket under my chair.

With some effort, Willa stoops to pick up the bird. My chair wobbles as she uses the back of it to pull herself upright again. How strange, she says, turning the bird over in her hands. Its head lolls like that of any dead thing. She tidies the colourful feathers. Ventures tentative fingers inside the cavity of its breast. So smooth, she says, and clean as cloth. She waggles unblooded fingers at me. How's it done?

That's beyond my ken, I say. It's Gothel's working.

Like your braid.

Like my braid.

The ring is in my apron pocket. Willa doesn't need to know about it. I keep chopping turnips until Boorma and Gryff arrive, breathing hard and brimming with questions. Boorma is keen to see the hollowed bird; Gryff refuses to touch it. He places a hand on my shoulder and gets down on one shaky knee. It's over, he says to me, isn't it? I don't look at him, not even when he puts his hand over mine, stilling the knife's work. Zel? It's over? She's dead?

I nod and he presses his cheek against the back of my hand. His whiskers are rough and scratchy. When he looks up again his eyes are wet. She'll come back now, he says and the hope in his voice hurts to hear. Gryff has always believed that Gothel had something to do with our daughter's leaving, that she wove a spell from afar to draw yet another girl to her tower. Nothing I've said in the past has convinced him otherwise. Nothing I say now would make a difference. I turn my hand to rub at his beard.

Gothel's death sits between us, and always will.

She's gone. She's gone and I'll never see her again. I'll never have the chance to scoop the forgiveness from my heart and offer it to her. I'll never know if she forgave me. There should have been more time. How can there be no more time?

A sob breaks in my throat. Gryff squeezes my hand and tells me that all will be well. We can stop looking over our shoulders now, he says. Gothel can do nothing more to hurt us.

My grief is a foreign thing, sharp and murky all at once. I haven't the first idea how to explain it — to my husband or to myself. Around my ankles, the braid tightens gently. I rest my head on Gryff's shoulder and let my tears run their course.

. . .

Despite what the stories say, Gothel didn't steal me.

The woman who carried me in her belly, who eventually birthed me 'neath the light of a near-full moon, was young and unmarried. It's true that she stole from Gothel's garden and that Gothel caught her. It's true that a bargain was struck, but not the one that people gossip on.

When Gothel spied the woman, barely older than Willa is now, plucking parsley in desperate handfuls for the third night in a row, she knew what was what. But it was too far late for the herb to have done her any good and, besides, the silly thing was eating it. Gothel had laughed when she'd told me that, but it wasn't a cruel laugh. Incredulous, indulgent even, but not cruel. Half-right can be worse than wrong, she'd said. Remember that.

Gothel might still have been able to help the young woman, then in her fourth moon and me not yet quickened within, but the risk was high. Instead, she told her to eat her fill of parsley — and furnished her as well with fresh eggs and salted pork and, when the cravings came, a basket of oranges that cost Gothel a small fortune in trade. In return, should the fates deem it proper, the woman was to bear the babe to term and Gothel would take care of matters then.

Don't think your mother didn't want you, Gothel often told me. She didn't know you, my darling. It was a baby she was so desperate to rid herself of, the notion of a baby and all that came after — and that's not the same as ridding herself of you. But you're *my* daughter, Rapunzel, as much as if you spilled from my own loins. Never doubt it.

Gothel had no desire for me to think myself unwanted and I never did. Not before my exile, at least.

Why she took me for herself, I'll never truly know. Maybe she didn't either.

Gryff insists that I'm naive, willfully blind even, where it concerns Gothel. I was a child, after all, and I only knew what Gothel wanted me to know. What mother would readily surrender her baby once it was born? The wise woman who'd sheltered me agreed. Unnatural, she said, a mother's love runs deepest of all — you've felt it yourself, girl. And I had, of course I had. The twins were my moon and my sun and I would have killed anyone who tried to take them from me.

I would have died for them.

But for all her faults, and the terrible things she has done, Gothel never once lied to me. I'm certain of that. Nor did she ever cast my birth mother as a villain. Neither strumpet nor slattern nor heartless wretch, simply a young woman with a burden too big to carry by herself. And this I know as well: not every woman yearns to be a mother, not even all those who already are. I've seen this for myself and make no judgement on them.

On most of them, in any case.

The men escorted me back to the village in silence, leading my chestnut gelding by his rein rope. I kept my hands in my lap, knotted into fists, and stopped asking questions after the first ones went unheeded. The narrow-faced man had simply instructed me to accompany them. The village circle required my presence, he'd said. I would not be harmed, he'd said. At that, Jacoby's face had tightened, his lips rolling to a thin line.

There were four of them. Tall men and broad.

I'd clenched my teeth and allowed them to take me.

The village was quiet. Laari, who normally greeted me with an excited grin before launching into a report of all that had happened since my previous visit, stood at the front of her cottage with water bucket in hand. She dropped her gaze as we passed, taking a sudden interest in the fraying hem of her apron. Nor would anyone else meet my eye, though several men exchanged nods with my captors. A woman whose name escaped me turned her shoulder away, hurriedly draping a corner of her shawl over the baby she held.

My heart beat hard against my ribs. This was not the village I knew. There was a brittleness to the air now. The tension of a breath held for too long.

On the outskirts, near where the trees grew thick and their

branches darkened the ground, stood three small round huts. They were fashioned from rough-hewn timber and their roofs were neatly thatched. The doors of two of the huts yawned open; the third's was held closed by a heavy wooden crossbar. There were no windows that I could see.

If you would, the narrow-faced man said. He gestured toward the nearest hut.

I thought the village circle wished to see me? I asked, not moving from my horse.

The narrow-faced man shook his head. I did not not say that. He gestured once again.

Four men, tall and broad.

I dismounted. Strode into the hut with my chin held high. Behind me, the door creaked shut. Its crossbar fell into place with a thunk. I closed my eyes, letting my sight adjust to the windowless dark, as the sound of hoof-beats receded into the distance. There was a mound of straw on one side of the hut — half gone to mould, by the smell — and an empty pot on the other. The last weak light of the evening filtered through the gaps between the timbers. I was glad for the season; in winter, the hut would freeze its luckless inhabitant to the marrow. I pushed at the door. It held fast. I hadn't really expected otherwise.

Resting my back against the wall, I took the small bag of pearl dust from my pocket. The weight of it in my palm was a comfort. The men had taken Heggu's sigil from me back at her cottage. Stamped it into the dirt and spat. Jacoby had made a sign of warding with his fingers. They hadn't searched my pockets, though. Hadn't seemed inclined to touch me at all.

What's happened here, Heggu? I muttered.

Night settled and the hut fell near to blackness. Would Gryff be worried when I didn't return, or would he assume I'd lingered late at the pearl house, drinking plum wine till my head was too muddled to ride back to camp? It wouldn't have been the first time I'd shared Heggu's bed; he likely wouldn't begin to fret until morning. At least I could rely on my chestnut gelding being cared for. Whatever fault the village had found with me, a good horse was too valuable a creature to be mistreated.

Choosing a spot away from the mouldy straw, I sat myself down to think.

Though I don't remember nodding off, I awakened with a start, all senses alert. A rough, rustling noise came from outside, followed by the scrape of wood on wood. I held my breath. More rustling, more scraping, and then the heavy thud of the crossbar hitting the ground. The door inched open, admitting a weak stream of moonlight, as my braid came snaking into the hut.

I could have wept, the relief was so great.

The braid wrapped itself around my waist and shoulders, nuzzled at the hollow of my throat. It quivered and hummed, as though each and every hair vibrated in the pleasure of finding me. I squeezed it tight. Pressed that golden, glossy hair to my mouth and whispered thanks, before disentangling myself from its coils and getting to my feet.

Scarce a dozen paces into the open, I paused. Turned to look at the other hut, the one with its door still closed and latched. The back of my neck itched. The braid bumped against my ankles, urging me forward. Hold a moment, I told it and marched across to the hut's door. The wood was rough beneath my knuckles. Who's in there, I asked, and rapped again.

There was a shuffling and then the sound of breathing, soft and close.

Who is it, I asked again. Speak if you wish to be free.

A sob, choked swiftly down. Zel? Is it you, Zel?

I lifted the crossbar and dropped it to the dirt, then pulled the door open. Meena, Jacoby's wife, was on her knees, her eyes hollowed and haunted. Come, I said, gesturing to the night outside. She shook her head, ground her lips hard together in a way that made me wince. Taking a deep breath, I leaned close. What is it, Meena? Why have they put you here?

The woman grasped my hands in both of hers. Bony fingers dug into my flesh, as she tried to pull me to my knees before her. We must be penitent, she said. We must show how penitent we are, and if we are penitent, if we are penitent, if we are penitent, we can walk again in the light.

It took many precious minutes to work the story loose.

Meena's baby had been born without breath. A boy, her first boy, he'd lain still and blue in her arms as she sobbed over his tiny body. Jacoby had been distraught at first, then withdrawn and distant. Only later, after Keeper Dorn had come to counsel him, did she find anger in her husband's eyes. Anger and disgust and something worse. I didn't know this Keeper Dorn but soon placed him as the narrow-faced man who'd led the party back at the pearl house. He'd come to the village at the end of the previous summer, Meena told me, bringing with him small items of trade and a recipe for a thick, fermented drink that several of the men took to sharing late at night. He brought words with him too, seductive and new, and a way of seeing the world by which some in the village began to abide.

They said it was because of me he died, Meena whispered.

I squeezed her hand. They're wrong. Some babies aren't for this world — that's the truth of it.

Shoulders slumped, the woman bowed her head. I told them it wasn't nothing, Zel, I told them. Just for the sickness, I told them, and nothing you hadn't given me before. My girls were all born, weren't they? Strong girls, pretty girls. I miss them, Zel, I miss them, I miss them — oh, we must be penitent.

It was Jacoby who'd brought the bottle of tonic to Keeper Dorn, along with the charm that Heggu had woven for Meena from dried lakeweed and which he'd found beneath his wife's pillow. Rough words had been slung from mouth to mouth. Witchcraft. Evil. Murder. When they'd gone to fetch Heggu, they'd found only her empty cottage.

The sacred balance was tilted out of true, Keeper Dorn had explained. The weight needed to be made up. On his instruction, the penitent huts had been built. With Meena locked in hers since late winter, I marvelled aloud that she hadn't frozen to death.

It's not *my* death that will balance things, she replied.

That's right, I said and tried to pull her to her feet. But a stubborn strength lingered in her wasted frame and she struggled against me, eventually falling limp and boneless to the ground. I begged her to leave with me. We could walk to my family's camp by dawn and be away from this place. She laughed at that, a harsh and empty sound that brought the taste of fear to my tongue.

They will have your family by now, Zel. Like they have mine. We must be penitent, penitent, penitent.

Stomach churning, I backed out of the hut. The pitiful woman pulled the door shut behind me but I refused to replace the crossbar, despite her pleas for me to do so. Instead, I returned to my own hut and sat cross-legged in the centre of the floor. My braid slid from the shadows and wove about me, nudging at my feet, my hips, growing more urgent with each passing moment. But as much as I wanted to believe otherwise, I knew that Meena was right. The village had known of our arrival. Another party of men would have been sent to collect Gryff and the twins and poor Boorma as well, most like, with her babe. A party larger than what came to fetch me — and armed, no doubt.

What would happen to my family once I was discovered gone?

And what did I suppose to do with my freedom?

I wasn't Heggu, solitary and self-sufficient. I could not run. I would not leave my children.

The braid wound itself around my shoulders and I hugged it close. Go, I whispered, keep yourself safe from sight; you will know when I need you again. After one final squeeze, it uncoiled and slipped from the hut with barely a sound. I left the door open. The sky was cloudless and, with the moon having travelled close to setting, the stars were bountiful. On their light, I made a solemn vow. Protection. Vengeance. Sacrifice. As needs demanded. The decision to stay was heavy on my chest, its uncertainty a suffocation.

(What if Meena was wrong?)

She wasn't.

(But what if?)

I shook my head and sat, straight-backed and silent, waiting for the new day to break and bring to bear what it would.

. . .

The moon is scarce more than a sliver and my breath frosts in the darkness. I don't need light to recognise Boorma's heavy tread as she approaches. Too cold to be out here, she says. Passes me a bowl of warm, spiced wine.

I won't sleep well tonight, I tell her.

She stands beside me, leaning against the goat pen, and we take turns sipping from the bowl. The animals are all huddled together, sharing their heat. A brown she-goat had gotten to her feet when I'd first arrived, bleating softly as she trotted over to greet me. Disappointed by my failure to bring food, she's settled back down with the rest of the flock now. Goats are pragmatic creatures. Sensible. I doubt they waste time dwelling on the past.

Boorma wants to know where we'll be going come spring, and I tell her that we haven't decided yet, Gryff and me. She knows he's reluctant and I suspect she'd rather we stayed in the valley as well. Her son, Maator, is clearly fond of Willa and my granddaughter's shown no sign of rebuffing him.

Not into the west, Boorma says.

I grit my teeth. Shake my head. There've been many tales passed around the mead hall this winter. The Keepers of the Balance are spreading their ways and their words through the foothills out west. We'll travel east, if we travel anywhere. Swing down to the south. There are trades we can make along those routes, and women who'll welcome my visits. I'll not go where Keepers tread, not so long as any I love in this world draw breath.

A sudden shiver rumbles through me. Wine splashes onto my gloved hand and Boorma takes the bowl, swallows what remains. Let's get your bones to bed, she says, before they freeze. We link arms and shuffle back to my yurt. Willa will already be chasing sleep and Gryff, I suspect, still tarrying at the mead hall. Smoke curls listlessly through the stovepipe; I'll need to stoke the fire with more dung before bedding down. Boorma gives me a rough hug then turns to leave.

I reach out and grab her by the sleeve. I thought I would see Gothel again, I say. I thought she would come find me.

Boorma touches my cheek, wipes at my tears with her glove.

I loved her, I say. I wanted her to know that.

She was your mother, Boorma tells me. She knew.

But I hated Gothel as well. Cursed her many times after being banished to the tower, though I had no skill in the practice and my muddling about with stolen hairs and furious words wrought no discernible effect. I cursed her to be struck down with boils and warts. I cursed her beloved garden to wither and die. I cursed her to fall from the tower as she climbed. The last, of course, committed without much thought for the consequences on my own imprisoned self.

There was a time one autumn when she didn't visit for more than a week. After five days my food was all but gone, though my water jug continued to replenish itself as usual. My only sanity was the brightly coloured bird that fluttered onto my windowsill each morning, bearing sprigs of berries or bushels of nuts or, once, a thin crust of bread. I was terrified that my curses had worked, that Gothel was dead and I would be trapped in the tower until I followed her at last to the grave.

When Gothel did finally return, I barely waited for her to climb into the room before exploding. I yelled at her, struck out with fists that she caught before their blows could land. Gently, she held me to her breast, pinning my arms to my sides until my rage abated.

You left me, I choked through my tears and snot. You abandoned me.

I would never abandon you, my darling. Did not my little friend come to visit? Did she not bring sustenance and sing my heartsong to you when I could not?

Gothel never told me where she had been, only that a matter of urgency had kept her away. It happened several more times over the years and each time my guts curdled with an anxious dread. I hated her for making me feel like that. I hated myself for the relief that swept my soul when she came back. For the meekness with which I lay my head in her lap while she unbraided my hair and combed the golden strands until they crackled and glowed. Occasionally, she took a pair of silver scissors from her pocket and snipped one or two to take with her when she left. Only Gothel could do that; not a single hair ever left my scalp without her permission.

I hated her, and I loved her, and I wanted to believe her when she said it was for my own protection that I was confined to the tower. The world was dangerous for girls my age, she said. There was magic in the flow of our blood, magic which would lure the danger close, and until I was a woman, until I was grown into my powers and had the cunning to know how to wield them, the tower would keep me safe.

Oh Gothel, you taught me so much and yet so little.

You taught me magic and herblore, but not the workings of my own body.

You taught me love, but said nothing of the intoxication of another's mouth on my own, another's hands on my skin, another's flesh pressed hot into mine.

You taught me how to watch the world from above, rather than walk within it.

But as much as Gryff would have me judge you, I refuse. Our twins — the grandchildren you never got to see, to hold, to know — our children who were raised on open plains and the backs of wagons, who rode a horse as soon as they could keep their balance, who slept with a starlit sky unfurled above them as often as they did tented roofs — oh, for all that freedom, would they have not been *safer* in a high, round room built from unyielding stone?

And might they not be with us now?

Keeper Dorn came to see me while the sun was still rising over the treeline. The two burly men who flanked him were clearly uneasy to see the hut with its door wide open. Even more so to find their captive unfled. Their leader revealed nothing, that narrow face calm and still. The three of them stopped a few paces away. Dorn nodded to me. When he spoke, his voice bore the gentle tones parents use when speaking to young children. You are what they say, then?

I'm not a witch, I told him.

Dorn tilted his head, his gaze travelling the length of my body. I did not move a single finger beneath his scrutiny, though my heart beat faster and my stomach clenched upon itself.

You gave Brother Jacoby's wife a witch's potion last summer, Dorn said.

I gave her a tonic, for the illness a pregnancy can bring.

Brother Jacoby's son was blue-born.

The one did not cause the other.

Dorn stared at me a moment longer before stepping in close, his movement so sudden and so fast that I cried out in surprise. He reached for a lock of my hair and gave it a light tug. Women should not wear their hair so short, he said. It is not balanced.

With that he turned and left, followed by one of the men. The other closed the door to the hut, repugnance twisting his face. I heard the crossbar fall and the creak of timber as he leaned his weight against the wall outside. I was not to be left alone again.

Almost three hours passed, to judge by the play of shadows along the ground, before I heard footsteps approach once more. Deep male voices muttered among themselves. Someone cursed. Then the crossbar was lifted and the door flung open. This time the men had chains — an expensive trade to have made — and I instinctively stepped back as they stepped inside.

She's afeared of the iron, like the Keeper said.

Bind her quick. Don't let her catch your eye.

There was no point in struggling. They wound a loop around my waist, threaded the ends of the chain through cuffs that were somewhat too large for my wrists. I squeezed my hands into fists to hide how easily I might be able to slip free. The men did not notice. One of them made a sign of warding and spat at my feet. The circle is waiting, he said.

I was led to the centre of the village, an open area where harvest fires were lit and marriages celebrated. And where the village circle met. There were no women among those gathered, which was strange. Discomforting. Sweat trickled down my back and I longed to scratch at it. They should think themselves lucky, these men, these cowards who do not deserve the name of men, that I am no witch. That I could not curse them.

Then I spied Gryff. Kneeling off to the side, hands bound with rope, face bloody and bruised. Our eyes met and he made to rise, but the broad-chested man standing behind him pushed him back down. The man carried a cudgel. Gryff lowered his head. His shoulders slumped. I had never seen him look so defeated. A sour taste coated my mouth and I swallowed hard, stumbling as one of my escorts pushed me forward to where Keeper Dorn was waiting. His narrow face seemed softened. There was an almost peaceful quality to his eyes, an upwards quirk to his lips.

For a moment, I felt hopeful. For a moment, all might still be well with the world.

Dorn lifted a hand to hush the murmur of the crowd. We serve the balance, he told them. In turn, the balance serves us. We are here to see it righted.

But when he turned to me, his gaze bore the chill of midwinter. Zel of the Tower, your actions have caused imbalance. A father has lost a son. This is a grave circumstance.

I glanced at Gryff. He wasn't looking at me. He wasn't looking at anyone.

Where are my children? I asked Dorn, hating the quaver in my voice.

Someone shoved me roughly from behind and I fell forward, chains clinking as I reached out to catch myself. But my restraints were drawn too short. I hit the ground hard, one shoulder rolling under me. There was a single cry from the crowd, quickly bitten off. It might have been Gryff. Dorn stepped forward and pulled to my feet. He admonished the man who pushed me, reminding him of the need to keep the balance, however difficult. Our female companion and her baby had been permitted to wait at our camp, Dorn told me, along with my daughter. They'd had no part in what had happened; they were not needed in the village. It was best they stayed away.

I could not breathe for all that was not said. Gryff still would not meet my eye. Others were only too keen to stare, their faces sharp and smug.

And my son, I croaked. Where is Will?

It wasn't anything that could be rightly called a smile, the thin, pallid thing that stretched Dorn's mouth so taut. A father lost a son, he reminded me. A boy-child was killed. It was an imbalance.

It was only when two men grabbed me by the arms that I realised I'd launched myself at the Keeper. Then kill *me*, I yelled at him, at the two who held me, at all those gathered around us. You believe I'm guilty of this sin, then avenge yourself on me. My son has done nothing; he is innocent. *He is innocent*.

The two men wrestled me to my knees. One of them snatched a fistful of my hair and pulled my head so far back I thought my neck would snap. Dorn stared down at me with a kind of pity. This isn't about sin, Zel of the Tower, or vengeance — the balance is all that concerns us. If it is not kept, then we walk in darkness as beasts.

I tried to speak once more, to beg again for my son's life, but Dorn held up his hand.

You do not understand, he said. This is not a trial. This is a witnessing.

It's difficult to remember all that happened next, and in what precise order. The door to a nearby cottage opened and Jacoby marched out, a sneer of triumph on his face. After him came two men, one I recognised as Laari's husband, transporting between them a limp, unmoving shape wrapped in a blanket. Will was only fourteen, and as slight as his sister. One man could have carried his body with little effort. They put him down, not ungently. Laari's husband, bending to tidy a corner of the blanket, flashed me a glance. His eyes were glossed with tears.

Rage and grief burst within me. I battled free and half-ran, half-crawled over to my son. Vaguely, I was aware of shouting around me and a harsh, broken bellow that a part of me knew to be Gryff's. But all I could think of was Will. I uncovered his face, his beautiful, perfect face which was still beautiful, still perfect, for all its terrible, irrevocable stillness. My son, I whispered, my darling, my boy.

I remember my throat closing over, my lungs seizing on airless space.

I remember the numbing, roaring silence filling my ears.

Most of all, I remember the agonised shriek that pulled me back to the world.

Dorn was lying on his back, a dark puddle seeping into the dirt from his side. Gryff was on the ground mere paces away, face down and struggling against the knees that dug into his back, keeping him from rising. And, inexplicably, there was Chance, right in the middle of the whole mess. A man had her about the waist, her arms pinned to her sides. She was twisting to free herself, kicking at anyone who got near. I called her name. Staggered to my feet.

Then I saw the knife fall from my daughter's hand.

What had she done, my Chance? My girl, so bright and bold. And whose death would serve balance this vengeful deed? Her own? Her father's? My mind cleared. My thoughts narrowed to a sure and certain focus.

I ran towards Dorn. Still on the ground, he'd propped himself up on elbow and hip to better see the wound. His face was pale. Jacoby blocked my path with a raised fist.

Let me pass, I said. If you want him to live.

Dorn called for Jacoby to stand aside which, after a small argument, he did. Should the Keeper die, he muttered as I pushed passed, I'll throttle you myself.

The wound was long but shallow, a slash more than a stab, and it was bleeding profusely. Clean edges, at least. Easy enough to stitch together. Gently, I prodded at the surrounding flesh. Dorn hissed. It burns, he said. It burns as fire does. Sweat ran down his face; his eyes were more red than white. I peered closer and my heart sank. Inside the wound, the tissue was tinged the subtle silver of winterfrost. I knew of only one thing that would cause such a symptom.

Later, my daughter would tell me how she waited until dark, waited until Boorma had finally worried herself to sleep, to sneak from the camp. Before she left, she took the small bottle of viper's wine from my healer's box and used it to coat the blade of her knife. She'd hidden all night in the village, tucked behind someone's woodbox, not knowing what had happened to her family but hopeful that morning would furnish her with answers. And a clear path. But the first she saw of her brother was when his body was delivered to the circle. She never stopped blaming herself, no matter how I tried to reason with her. If only she'd searched for him. If only she'd found him. If only they'd escaped. If only, if only — my daughter is expert at that game.

Viper's wine is useful in so many ways. A drop mixed in various tinctures and teas can help with troubled sleep, or stopped-up bowels, or twinges in the heart; alone and without dilution, it's a deadly poison. An open wound exposed to viper's wine will turn brittle and waste, the flesh will break down, the body will eat itself alive. It is the slowest of tortures.

I swivelled to see Chance now crouched on the ground, one man twisting her arms cruelly behind her back. Blood rushed to my cheeks. Fingernails dug into my palm. It took all that was left of my will not to run to my daughter, not to scratch out the eyes of her captor and trample them into the dirt. Chance met my gaze; a ghost of a smile tripped across her mouth. Pale, frightened and yet — triumphant.

I turned back to Dorn, to the circle of men crowded around us. He needs to be out of the sun, I told them. Dorn quieted the resulting growls with a wave of his hand. Listen to her, he said. The mother can balance the daughter's work. I've no idea if he really believed such a thing but he must have realised he'd suffered no ordinary injury. As the men lifted him, the Keeper groaned and clamped a sweat-slicked hand around my arm. The daughter will be held forfeit, he said, loud enough for all to hear. The father as well.

Dorn's home was little bigger than the penitent huts, and windowless. As the Keeper was lowered onto his bed pallet, Jacoby pushed me up against the wall. You're all going to die, he whispered, his breath hot in my ear. But I will make sure to give your witch-daughter a fine send-off.

I dug my nails so hard into my palm, they drew blood.

Once all the men had left, all but Jacoby who took up a

position beside the door, the Keeper rolled his yellowing eyes toward me. How long, he asked. I told him that I wasn't sure. Until dawn perhaps, or perhaps sooner, but if I could retrieve some ingredients from camp then—

There'll be none of your witchcraft here, Jacoby interrupted.

Will it help, Dorn asked?

Perhaps, I said. He knew I was lying. With the viper's wine spreading through his body, there was nothing I could do apart from administering opium to quell the pain — and even that would only work for so long. In truth, I'd wanted the time to think. There must be a trade that would vouchsafe the lives of my daughter and my husband, some bargain I could strike. But it needed to be done while Dorn still drew breath enough to command it. Once he was dead . . . I cast a surreptitious glance toward Jacoby. The man's eyes were flat and dark. His hand clenched and unclenched around the cudgel he carried.

At least he was in here, with me, and not standing guard over my daughter.

The day wore on. Water was brought for me to wash the wound, and vinegar too. Needle and thread were fetched, my chains unshackled and, more for appearances sake than anything else, I stitched the wound closed. The bleeding stopped but the spread of silver was visible under his skin. Beautiful, in its own terrible way. I wiped Dorn's face with a sodden rag and squeezed drops into his mouth whenever he seemed lucid enough to swallow. Fire, he kept murmuring, my blood is aflame. I kept hoping for another man to relieve Jacoby of his watch, someone like Laari's husband perhaps, a man more open to reason, or even compassion, but all who came to the door were sent away.

We were to keep vigil alone then, Jacoby and me. I sat in my chair at Dorn's side. He remained in his place by the door. We didn't look at each other.

As night fell, I began to hum softly. It was a bedtime song I used to sing to the twins when they were very young. It hurt to remember how Will would try to sing along, giggling and making up his own words. Jacoby, slumped now on the floor, growled for me to shut up, but Dorn reached out and clasped my hand in his.

See, I said to Jacoby, it is a comfort to him.

He said nothing more. I continued to hum, low and lilting, spying sidelong at my guard in the candlelight. After a while, the man's head drooped to his chest. His breathing deepened. I hummed on, waiting, waiting. Finally, there came a feather-light brush of hair against my ankle. I looked down and my lullaby faltered. Jacoby snuffled loudly in his sleep, just once, before I forced myself to pick up the tune.

My braid had found a way into the Keeper's hut. Only, not as my braid.

Through every slim crack or knothole, loose stands of hair slipped in through the walls and curved their golden, glowing path across the floor. Tears pricked at my eyes. For if this was the *only* way my braid could enter without notice, it meant there was no escape to be made. Men must be keeping too close and wakeful a watch outside, even at this late hour.

Hairs curled around my fingers, my wrist, wound right up to my throat. More of them converged to make a spiral in my lap, quivering as I stroked them. I stared at the needle I'd left on the small table beside the bed. At the coarse thread I'd used to close up Dorn's side. It might be too late. It was probably too late. And yet.

Bending close to the wound, I sawed one of the stitches back and forth between my teeth until at last it snapped, then carefully picked the rest free. The stench was terrible. Sour and acrid, not the smell of rotting flesh so much as bitter greens left to drown in a sodden field. Still humming, I gathered a handful of loose hairs and rolled them together as I would stuffing for a rag doll. Then I held apart the edges of the wound and pushed the bundle inside.

Dorn gasped and arched his back but did not appear to waken.

Neither did Jacoby, over at his post by the door.

It took three attempts to thread a single hair through the needle, my hands shook so much. But finally I managed it and, by the flickering candlelight, I stitched Dorn up again. His skin rippled, or the flesh beneath it did, and grew so hot I could feel the fever from where I sat. Please, I whispered, oh please. I wiped the cool, wet cloth over his face and chest. Steam hissed into the air. The Keeper arched his back again, tossed himself from side to side so vigorously he would have fallen from his pallet had I not thrown my body over his.

Jacoby startled from sleep, scrambled to his feet. What happens here, he demanded. Is this death come to claim me? He spoke the last too eagerly, or so it seemed.

No, I snapped. This is death taking her leave of you.

By break of dawn, the Keeper was able to sit up and drink from a bowl of mutton broth while several of the village circle gathered to examine him. The wound was healing to a reddish, puckered line that itched, he said, but no longer burned. His skin was still clammy to the touch, but cool, and a healthy flush of colour was returning to his face. There was no sign of the thin golden hair I'd stitched into his side, nor of any else left inside the hut.

She spelled you, Jacoby insisted. It was witchcraft and no good can come of it.

The balance has been kept, Dorn replied. But there was a fearful new light in his eyes when he looked at me, and he would not hold my gaze for long. Fetch her people, he told the circle. They are no longer forfeit.

As long as I might live, I shall never again see anything as beautiful as my daughter's face that morning as she was led into the centre of the village where I'd been made to wait. Grubby and red-eyed, her long brown hair tangled and snarled, but alive, oh blessed by three, my darling Chance, *alive*. Gryff walked by her side, one arm tight around her shoulders. His face appeared neutral but I could see the tightness in his jaw from where I stood and I knew the small vein in his temple would be throbbing fit to burst.

Jacoby dug his fingers into my arm one last time before letting me go. Witch, he hissed, shoving me forward. Though weak with hunger and trepidation, I forced myself to keep to a steady walk, first one foot and then the other, chin jutted high. The men of the village pressed closed, watching. Some, like Jacoby, wore murderous scowls; others seemed merely fearful. I was put in mind of the packs of half-wild dogs that roam the outskirts of the larger townships in the south, seldom a danger unless you were foolish enough to run from them, or tempt them with uncovered meat, raw and dripping.

Or if you had the misfortune to be a child. Isolated and vulnerable.

When I reached my daughter, I stooped to hug her but she stiffened in my arms, her shoulders sharp and stubborn. Gryff took hold of my hand and brought it to his lips. His eyes were hollow. My love, I said to him, we must go while we can. Please.

Dorn escorted us from the village himself, followed by Jacoby and a dozen or so men. All the cottage doors we passed were shut; the few windows curtained and blind. I imagined all the women locked behind those door, children pressed into their skirts. Forbidden to look upon the witch in their midst lest they become likewise corrupted. Lest they be banished to the penitent hut along with Jacoby's poor wife. I kept hold of Chance's hand. Squeezed it so tight that a small, plaintive sound escaped her throat. Hush, I said. I loosened my grip but did not let go. I thought I would never let go of her again.

At last we came to the tether-line, where my chestnut gelding waited, tossing his head and fretting over the terrible burden that had been roped across his saddle. Gryff stopped in his tracks. I could hear his teeth grinding together at the sight of that motionless, blanket-wrapped form. He half-turned and I stepped in front of him, keeping myself between my husband and Dorn. Grabbing his chin with my free hand, I forced him to look at me. To see me.

You cannot, I whispered. We still have one child — would you leave your daughter fatherless?

His eyes gleamed. His face was flushed. It would take so very little to spark him.

You will leave this village and its lands, Dorn said. We will not suffer you here again.

Behind him, Jacoby raised his voice. *She* should not be allowed to leave. My son is murdered.

Dorn nodded toward the tether-line. The balance has been righted, Brother Jacoby. Would you set it off its kilter once again?

She should be made penitent, Jacoby retorted, pointing at me. Around him, other men began to mutter words of assent.

I pushed my daughter behind me, felt Gryff move forward. Blood rushed through my ears. Get Chance away from here, I whispered. Protect her.

Gryff's hand gripped my shoulder. I wanted to sink beneath its strength. No, Zel, he muttered, his breath warm in my hair. I will protect you both.

Brothers! Dorn raised his hand. She is not a member of our village; the penitence is not hers to take. One by one, he turned to look at the men. Held their gaze until they dropped it. Seeing the battle lost, Jacoby swore and kicked viciously at the ground. I do not doubt it was my face he imagined crushed beneath his boot.

Alone, Dorn took us the remaining distance to the tetherline. He untied the chestnut gelding's rein-rope and handed it to Gryff. Pack up your camp with haste, he said, glancing up at the noonday sky. It will be best if you are far from here once it is night. There are some who find a brutal freedom in the darkness.

The twins had been close, inseparable, indivisible. The death of her brother was a wound Chance carried always. Worse than viper's wine, and even slower to wend its way through her veins. He was my heart, Mama, she screamed at me once. They cut out my heart and you did nothing. Worse than nothing — you *saved* the man who murdered him.

Perhaps I should have told her what I actually did afterwards. If I had, she might have found some solace in it. If I had, she might still be here with us, with Willa. I wasn't ashamed — I'm *still* not ashamed — but neither was I proud. The comfort that vengeance offers is a hollow one; I did not want to teach my daughter otherwise.

My hair had found its way back to the camp before we did, scruffy and dishevelled, but braided together once more. Boorma was overcome to see us, ecstatic and then distraught, and we all wept together as we packed up our belongings and loaded the wagon. Will, we would farewell the next day, with many miles between us and the village where his death had come for him. A grave dug beneath an ancient tree. His body nestled within the roots.

(Earth take you, my child, my son. Earth take you, and goddess keep you.)

That first night, while Gryff kept a jaw-tight watch, I undid my braid and brushed that wave of golden hair until it shone. Then I plaited it tightly together again, smooth and glossy and sleek, and hugged it close. Go, I told it, go and finish this.

It was several days before the braid found us again. I gathered the warm, sluggish weight of it into my arms and felt no different. Not better, not worse. The stone that had been pressed against my chest since my son's death remained solid, immovable; for the first time, I found myself thinking of Jacoby with something other than loathing.

We wintered deep in the south that year, deep in our grief. Strange stories followed in our tracks, were traded in the mead hall and grew ever taller in the telling. A village out east where all the menfolk had died in a single night. Strangled, or so it looked, with several of them chafed red about the throat — but how could such a thing be done? It was a plague, people said, or a punishment. It was the women who did it and made up fancies to cover themselves. It was a a lie, made up to scare credulous children.

Do you think them all dead, Gryff asked me late one night, his voice lowered and hoarse.

I looked over at Chance, curled into a ball on her sleeping pad.

Would you weep for them if they were, I asked my husband. He didn't answer, just pulled me close and kissed the back of my neck. I relaxed into his embrace, ran my hands over his skin. It had been a long time. His body felt different. Sharper in some places, softer in others. Wordless, breath hot between our mouths, we moved together. Found ourselves, each other.

We never again spoke of the village, or the vengeance my braid had wrought there.

The following spring, Boorma told us she would be staying in the valley. She'd cleaved to a local horse breeder, a good man whose eyes brightened with adoration whenever their gaze lit upon her. He loved both of her children as well, and said he would teach Maator how to bring young horses to the saddle, and how to keep a breedline strong.

Chance never found her balance.

She drifted along with us, stoic and mostly silent. There were many she took a tumble with, once she came into her womanhood, but none to whom she cleaved. Not even for a season. When her bloods stopped, she couldn't say for certain who sowed the seeds. Couldn't say, or maybe just wouldn't. As her belly rounded, a light returned to her eyes. A certain hopefulness, sometimes even joy. I hadn't seen her look that way for many years. Not since that awful summer. Not since Will. And I allowed myself to hope as well. That Chance was returning to us. That this small new life would bring her back.

What a fool I was to think it.

There'll be no snow today. The sky is a pale, sparrow-egg blue and stretches cloudless and clear across the valley. Gryff has gone to tend to the dark bay mare. Willa is still in bed, snoring gently. The bigger her belly gets, the more trouble she has getting to sleep at night and we don't like to rouse her too early in the morning. There'll be enough of that when the baby comes.

The baby. My great-granddaughter. My daughter's granddaughter.

I thought I could do it, Chance told me. Willa, scarcely eight moons old, lay settled in her arms. But this is too big, Mama. I look at her and I see him, I feel his death all over again. I love her so much, Mama, but the love, it claws me up inside and I can't . . . *I can't.*

I didn't listen, I didn't *hear*, and a week later she packed herself a travel-sack.

Don't think you can crawl back here, I snapped when she came to say goodbye. We'll raise your daughter, your father and me, of course we will. But if you walk away now, Chancey-girl — if you abandon this child of yours like she's an old toy you've grown tired of playing with — then don't dare call yourself her mother.

All these years later and those words, the last I ever spoke to my daughter, hook fresh in my heart. I'd been furious, frightened and half-sick with the shock of it, but by the time I'd calmed down she was gone. My Chance is clever and, moreover, as stubborn as I am. If she doesn't want to be found, she won't be — not by any common means, at least.

In my hands, the brightly coloured bird is limp. I smooth its plumage with my thumb and turn it over so that the cavity in its breast falls open. The space is small but there's room enough to hold what I need.

A long, thin plait made from three strands of golden hair, wound to a neat coil.

Petals from a white tulip, dried and pressed. I would have preferred a fresh bloom but it's not the season. Chance knows her herblore; she will understand the meaning.

And my words, my whispered plea: *forgive me, daughter; you never left my heart.*

The braid stirs sluggishly at my feet. There's silver winding through the gold now, more and more with each passing hour. I tug at the end of a single strand, still brassy-bright, and it comes loose willingly, threads itself through the needle with swift and eager speed. It's but the work of a dozen stitches to sew up the bird and, as I tie the last one off, the creature begins to flutter in my hand. Its eyes are bright onyx jewels.

I set it upright, watch as it flits to the back of my chair and begins to preen.

Reaching down, I run my hand over the braid. It's almost wholly silver now and makes only the slightest response to my touch. I want to offer thanks but my throat closes on the words. They are not enough, they are not nearly enough. Still, I try to believe that what Boorma says is true: Gothel was my mother, and she will know. Wherever she is, she will know.

As soon as I open the door, the bird finds its wings. It makes a swooping circle of the yurt then darts past me, trilling joyfully. I watch it fly, a speck of colour against all that the limitless blue, until it's gone too far for my old eyes to follow. In her bed, Willa stirs. Who's there, Mother Zel?

I close the door against the cold. A messenger, I tell her. Go back to sleep.

I can't, she groans. The little one's turning somersaults.

That's a good sign, I say. She'll be healthy and strong. She'll ride before she can walk.

Smiling, Willa beckons me over. I sit on the edge of the bed, my hand pressed to her belly, and laugh as a tiny foot kicks at my palm.

Can we stay on this spring, Willa asks. Just for the spring? Boorma says we'd be welcome.

I recognise her mother in the shy, hopeful way she tilts her head. Her mother as a young girl, before the terrible summer that quelled the light in her eyes for good.

Just for the spring, I tell her. Willa grins and I feel the baby within her kick once more.

ABOUT THE AUTHOR

Photo by Paul Ewins

Kirstyn McDermott has been working in the darker alleyways of speculative fiction for much of her career. She is the author of two award-winning novels, *Madigan Mine* and *Perfections*, and a collection of short fiction, *Caution: Contains Small Parts*. Her stories and poetry have been published in various magazines, journals and anthologies both within Australia and internationally, with her most recent work being *Never Afters*, a series of novellas that retell classic fairy tales. She holds a PhD in creative writing with a research focus on re-visioned fairy tales and produces and co-hosts a literary discussion podcast, The Writer and the Critic. Kirstyn lives in Ballarat, Australia, with fellow writer Jason Nahrung and two distinctly non-literary felines. She can be found online at www.kirstynmcdermott.com.

ALSO BY KIRSTYN MCDERMOTT

Perfections

Madigan Mine

Caution: Contains Small Parts

Triquetra

THANK YOU FOR BUYING THIS BRAIN JAR PRESS CHAPBOOK

To receive special offers, bonus content, and info on new releases and other great reads, visit us online at www.BrainJarPress.com